PUFFIN BOOKS

The Super-Roo of Mungal(

Super-Roo is the Head Animal at the wonderful Willawallawalla Waterhole at the foot of the purple and pink Mungalongaloo Mountains. One of his jobs is to keep out human polluters and foreign animals — even if they are famous explorers on pedigree camels.

So when the great McGurk and his Afghan camel brave the dreaded Deadibone Desert on their epic quest of discovery, they are to find that the dead centre holds secrets more amazing than they could ever have imagined.

Osmar White has himself travelled widely throughout Australia and written much about it. Jeff Hook is well known for his cartoons, which appear in many Australian newspapers, especially the Melbourne *Sun*.

Osmar White

The Super-Roo
of Mungalongaloo

Illustrated by Jeff Hook

Puffin Books

Puffin Books, Penguin Books Australia Ltd,
487 Maroondah Highway, P.O. Box 257
Ringwood, Victoria, 3134, Australia
Penguin Books Ltd,
Harmondsworth, Middlesex, England
Penguin Books,
625 Madison Avenue, New York, N.Y. 10022, U.S.A.
Penguin Books Canada Ltd,
2801 John Street, Markham, Ontario, Canada
Penguin Books (N.Z.) Ltd,
182-190 Wairau Road, Auckland 10, New Zealand

First published by Wren Publishing Pty Ltd 1973
Published in Puffin Books 1978
Reprinted 1979, 1980, 1981

Text copyright © Osmar White, 1973, 1978
Illustrations copyright © Jeff Hook, 1973, 1978

Made and printed in Hong Kong by
Sheck Wah Tong Printing Press Ltd

CIP

White, Osmar.
The super-roo of Mungalongaloo.

For children
ISBN 0 14 031110 6

I. Hook, Geoffrey, illus. II. Title.

A823'.3

Contents

CHAPTER ONE   9

In which the Intrepid Explorer McGurk Prepares for his Expedition into the Dreaded Deadibone Desert

CHAPTER TWO   16

In which McGurk and his Camel Run Out of Water but Are Saved by Backward-flying Budgerigars and a Keen Sense of Smell

CHAPTER THREE   25

In which our Valiant Adventurers Meet the Most Terrific Kicker in the World and Are Threatened with Immediate Expulsion

CHAPTER FOUR   35
*In which Super-Roo is Much Taken with McGurk's Super
Sporran and McGurk is Taken for a Super Ride*

CHAPTER FIVE   46
*In which the Council of Animals Rule to Exterminate
McGurk and his Camel, and Super-Roo has to do some
Super-quick Thinking*

CHAPTER SIX   57
*In which our Heroes Travel Long and Hard, to Return
Triumphantly and Declare they Discovered Nothing
(except a Secret)*

1

*In which the Intrepid Explorer McGurk Prepares for his
Expedition into the Dreaded Deadibone Desert*

Away out in the Mungalongaloo Mountains in the
middle of Australia, where the jaggedy peaks are all
purple and primrose and pink and prune-coloured,
there is a wonderful waterhole called Willawallawalla.

Willawallawalla is the only waterhole for hundreds
and hundreds of miles.

It is in the dead centre of the dreaded Deadibone
Desert.

The Deadibone Desert is an awful place. In the
daytime the weather is so hot that the emus lay hard-
boiled eggs. In the night-time the weather is so cold
that the frogs wear jumpers to keep them from freezing
to death.

For hundreds and thousands and millions of years
nobody knew that the Mungalongaloo Mountains were
in the dead centre of the Deadibone Desert. They had
not been discovered.

One day, not very long ago, a very famous and brave explorer named Dr Alastair Angus Archibald McGurk M.D. went out to the middle of Australia looking for new places to explore.

When he got there, the people said to him, 'Don't be silly. All the places in the middle of Australia have been explored already.'

Dr McGurk said, 'But what about the dreaded Deadibone Desert? I bet that hasn't been explored!'

'Of course it hasn't,' the people said. 'The Deadibone Desert doesn't count. It is so *awful* - so hot in the day-time and so cold in the night-time - that it will never be explored.'

'Hoots and toots!' exclaimed Dr McGurk, who was a Scotsman. 'That's the very kind of place I have been looking for. I will send to Afghanistan for my special champion pedigree double-humped riding camel. Her name is Cathie Khan. She has beautiful brown eyes and long silky eyelashes. I bet you twenty cents I can ride her right across the Deadibone Desert from east to west.'

'We bet you twenty cents you can't,' the people said. 'It has been a dry season. It hasn't rained for twenty-seven years and four months and the weather people on television say no change is in sight.'

11

But brave Dr McGurk did not care what the people said. He was sure Cathie Khan could carry him across the desert. He sent to Afghanistan for her and, while he was waiting, he went into training to get fit.

He gave up drinking water until five o'clock in the afternoon and he had nothing to eat but dry biscuits and salt salami sausage. When it was a cold night he pulled all the blankets off his bed and slept in his trews.

When it was a hot day he put on five pullovers and ran eight kilometres.

By the time Cathie Khan arrived, Dr McGurk was very fit. He was ready for his long, dangerous ride across the Deadibone Desert.

Cathie Khan came from Afghanistan by air. She had never been in an aeroplane before and the flight upset her. When Dr McGurk led her off, she was shivering all over. She was suffering from jet jitters.

Dr McGurk gave her a dose of soothing syrup and told her to rest for three days.

On the fourth day she felt much better. She got up and, for breakfast, drank one hundred and ten litres of water, and ate four bales of hay, one bag of oats and a banana.

Dr McGurk put on his exploring clothes: snake-proof stockings, thorn-proof kilt, scorpion-proof trews, a bush shirt, hob-nailed shoes and his tam-o'-shanter with cork bobbles on top. Last of all he buckled on his belt and sporran.

When he was dressed, Dr McGurk made Cathie Khan kneel down. He loaded her front hump with packets of porridge and dry biscuits and salt salami sausage. Then he filled a big water bag and hung it round her neck. Last of all, he put a saddle on her back hump, climbed up on it and cried: *'Atcha, atcha, imshi!'* which is Afghan for 'Okay, let's go!'

Cathie didn't want to get up. She moaned and groaned and rumbled and grumbled, but at last Dr McGurk got her moving. He gave her a good spank and shouted 'Heave-ho! Hup!'

All the people and their dogs came out of the houses to watch Dr McGurk set out on his great adventure. He sat up very proudly in the saddle on Cathie's back hump and played a tune called *Flowers of the Forest* on his bagpipes.

Some of the people cheered because they thought he was very brave. Some of them cried because they thought he would never come back alive. Rude children called out: 'Mad McGurk, Mad McGurk, yah-yah-*yah!*' But the dogs howled because the bagpipe music hurt their ears.

Soon Dr McGurk and Cathie disappeared into the big cloud of red dust that always hangs over the Deadibone Desert.

2

In which McGurk and his Camel Run Out of Water but Are Saved by Backward-flying Budgerigars and a Keen Sense of Smell

On they went. On and on and on...over the spiny spinifex grass and through the miserable mulga scrub and across the glittering gibber-gibber plains covered with shiny black rocks. They crossed salt-pans and clay-pans. Sometimes they saw mirages.

The Deadibone Desert was twice as awful as people said it was, but Dr McGurk did not worry. He was quite sure Cathie Khan could carry him right across it.

In the evening when the sun went down, Dr McGurk called out: 'Whoa, whoa there, Cathie! Kneel doon, ma bonnie wee lassie!' Cathie, who understood the Scottish language as well as the Afghan language, stopped and knelt down.

Dr McGurk got out of the saddle and unloaded the gear on Cathie's front hump to make camp. He listened to his transistor radio for the news and the weather report. It wasn't a day of Total Fire Ban so he lit a fire

and cooked his supper of porridge and salt salami sausage. If it had been a day of Total Fire Ban he would just have munched dry biscuits.

After supper Dr McGurk took two sips of water from the water bag and marched round and round playing his bagpipes to keep his spirits up.

Cathie lay down and rumbled and grumbled and gurgled and pumped the water round inside her.

At nine o'clock Dr McGurk set his alarm clock and said his prayers. Then he wrapped himself in his tartan rug and lay down on the ground. Soon he and Cathie were fast asleep.

For twenty-seven days Dr McGurk and Cathie travelled across the Deadibone Desert and in all that time they did not see a single living thing. What was worse, they couldn't find any water.

Cathie's humps started to shrink. They got smaller and smaller. At night she no longer pumped water round inside her because there was no longer any water left to pump.

Dr McGurk was thirsty too. He had only one sip out of the water bag after supper and only half a sip after breakfast.

At last the water bag was dry, except for about three sips which he decided to keep for an emergency, for they were not even half way across the Deadibone Desert. He was getting worried about Cathie. She was so thirsty she started to cry. The tears rolled down her silky eyelashes and plopped on to the hot sand and sizzled.

Dr McGurk was very sorry for her. He was a kind man, but he knew he must not show he was worried or she might become hysterical and have a camel tantrum. He slapped her tail and said gruffly: 'Och, stop your crying, you silly animal! You're wasting water!'

To make it easier for her, he climbed down off her back and walked beside her, singing 'The camels are coming, hooray, hooray!', to cheer her up.

That night they camped under a dead snakewood tree. Poor Cathie was so exhausted she just lay on her back with her legs sticking up in the air, giving out great dry sobs. Dr McGurk was so worried about her and he could not sleep at all.

Dr McGurk got up specially early next morning. He knew he would have to do something to save Cathie and himself. He took his telescope and climbed to the top branch of the dead snakewood tree and looked all around.

There, jutting up on the skyline, he saw the purple and primrose and pink and prune-coloured peaks *of the Mungalongaloo Mountains!*

Dr McGurk was so excited he nearly fell out of the snakewood tree. 'Whirrawhirroo, hooray, hurroo!' he shouted in a croaky voice, 'We're saved!'

But they weren't saved yet. The Mungalongaloo Mountains were still fifty kilometres away. Dr McGurk and Cathie stumbled across the scorching sand under the searing sun.

The sun set and the stars came out, but Dr McGurk dared not stop. He knew that if Cathie got down she would never have strength to stand up again.

They walked all through the night. Their tongues were hanging out and they had headaches. Their feet were blistered and they itched all over - but they did not stop. They walked on and on and on. Sometimes

Cathie stumbled because her tired legs were so wobbly, but Dr McGurk cried: 'Heave-ho! Hup! None of that, now!'

When dawn came, two raggedy black crows dropped out of the sky and flew round in circles calling out: 'Poor show! Poor show! Poor sho-o-w!'

Then Dr McGurk saw a big flock of green budgerigars flying backwards. The budgerigars in the Deadibone Desert are called garbudgeries because they always fly backwards to keep the dust out of their eyes.

Dr McGurk did a Highland Fling for joy. With all this birdlife about, he realized there must be water nearby.

3

In which our Valiant Adventurers Meet the Most Terrific Kicker in the World and Are Threatened with Immediate Expulsion

It was Cathie who actually found it. Camels can smell water from a long way off. Her knees stopped wobbling. She threw up her head. She sniffed. Then she gave a great snort and she bolted.

'Stop, stop!' Dr McGurk cried, running after her as fast as he could. 'Wait for me, Cathie!'

But Cathie would not stop. She headed straight for the Willawallawalla Waterhole and jumped into it. By the time Dr McGurk caught her, she had drunk three hundred and fourteen litres and fifteen millilitres of water - and swallowed a fish by mistake.

Dr McGurk knew that she could get a terrible stomach-ache from drinking fast after being so thirsty, but it was too late to tell Cathie to control herself.

So he also drank the cool green water and sat down on the bank to rest awhile.

When he had rested, he took off his shoes and his socks and his shirt and his kilt and his tam-o'-shanter with cork bobbles on top, and went for a paddle. He was just about to swim when he heard a great big, rough, gruff, furry voice say: *'You there! What do you think you are doing, polluting that pool!'*

Dr McGurk nearly jumped out of his undershirt with surprise. He whirled around. Nobody was there!

Then he saw a huge red kangaroo sitting under the shade of a coolabah tree beside the waterhole. Suddenly it bounded towards him. It was the biggest kangaroo Dr McGurk had ever seen. It was about four metres tall.

It stopped right in front of Dr McGurk and said in its great big, rough, gruff, furry voice: 'Be off with you, you horrible human being - and take that galumphing, double-humped, fish-eating camel with you. We don't want polluters paddling in this waterhole. How would you like it if kangaroos and other animals washed their feet in your drinking water?'

'Good grief!' gasped Dr McGurk. 'It's a talking kangaroo! I must be suffering from sunstroke and heat exhaustion and hallucinations!'

'You'll be suffering from a lot worse if you don't catch that camel and get out of here,' the big red kangaroo said crossly.

'Great grief!' groaned Dr McGurk. 'All this hardship must have driven me daft! Kangaroos can't talk!'

'Well, *this* one can,' said the big kangaroo. 'Who are you and what are you doing here?'

'My name is Alastair Angus Archibald McGurk M.D.,' Dr McGurk said with dignity. 'I am a famous explorer and I am riding across the dreaded Deadibone Desert on my camel Cathie Khan. Who are you?'

The big red kangaroo puffed out his chest proudly. 'I am Super-Roo,' he said. 'I am Head Animal at Willa-wallawalla Waterhole and everybody has to do what I say.'

Super-Roo sounded so bossy that Dr McGurk began to get cross. 'Is that so?' he said. 'Tell me, apart from being able to talk, what makes you so super? You look pretty ordinary to me.'

'I'll have you know,' said Super-Roo, 'that when I'm hopping uphill I can hop two kilometres in a single hop. When I'm hopping downhill I can hop four kilometres. When I'm hopping on the flat I can hop three kilometres at a single hop. I am three metres forty centimetres high and my tail is two metres long. I weigh half a tonne and I

am the most terrific kicker in the world. Once I kicked a water buffalo from just there, where you are standing, right up to the top of that prune-coloured peak you can see.'

'Why did you kick the poor thing?' asked Dr McGurk.

'Because it was wallowing,' Super-Roo said. 'And it wasn't a poor thing. It was a buffalo. Willawallawalla Waterhole is a wildlife sanctuary for Australian animals only. No other sorts of animals are allowed. Human beings aren't allowed either.'

Dr McGurk lost his temper because Super-Roo was so rude.

'Oh, hold your whist, you bragging, boastful beastie!' he snapped. 'I'll no' go till I'm good and ready. If you try to kick me, I will get my big-game gun and shoot you.'

'Pooh to you,' said Super-Roo. 'Guns don't hurt me. I'm bullet-proof.'

'Nonsense,' said McGurk. 'What makes you think you're bullet-proof?'

'I know I am,' said Super-Roo. 'Only last year Petfood Pete tried to shoot me with his high-powered, double-barrelled, kangaroo-shooting, repeater rifle, and the bullets just bounced off me.'

'Who is Petfood Pete?' asked Dr McGurk.

'Oh, he's just another human being,' Super-Roo replied. 'But nastier than most. He shot kangaroos to make them into pet food.'

'Well, *I* don't shoot kangaroos to make them into pet food,' barked Dr McGurk. 'I'll thank you to keep a civil tongue in your head when you're talking to me.'

'Put on your skirt and catch your camel,' Super-Roo barked back. 'Go away and go quietly, or I'll kick you twice as far as I kicked Petfood Pete.'

By now Dr McGurk was really furious, not so much about the kicking but because Super-Roo had called his kilt a skirt.

'It's not a skirt, it's a *kilt,* you ignorant animal,' he shouted. 'Maybe you are three metres forty centimetres high and maybe you are bullet-proof. But I don't think much of you. Kangaroos are supposed to be kind, gentle animals. You're not. You are just an overgrown, selfish bully!'

Super-Roo was quite surprised at being spoken to in this way. 'Look,' he said in a much more gentle voice. 'I'm only doing my job as Head Animal. The rules of this waterhole say that human beings and camels are not allowed.'

'Do you mean that just because you have some silly rule, you are going to kick us out to die of thirst in the Deadibone Desert? We must have rest and Cathie must have time for her humps to fill out again,' Dr McGurk said rather anxiously.

Super-Roo sat back on his tail and thought.

4

In which Super-Roo is Much Taken with McGurk's Super Sporran and McGurk is Taken for a Super Ride

While he was thinking, Dr McGurk put on his clothes. He was buckling on his belt and sporran when Super-Roo stopped thinking and stared. 'What's that thing you've got hanging down in front of your kilt?' he asked.

'It is my sporran, of course,' said Dr McGurk.

'What is it for?' Super-Roo asked.

'It's a wee pouch to keep things in,' answered Dr McGurk.

Super-Roo bent over and looked closely at Dr McGurk's sporran. He pulled it open with his paw and felt inside it.

'Stop that!' Dr McGurk said sternly. 'You're tickling! A body would think you had never seen a sporran before!'

'Well, I never have,' said Super-Roo. 'But it's the very thing!'

'The very thing...for what?' Dr McGurk asked.

'To carry my little son Joey in,' Super-Roo replied.

'Humph!' Dr McGurk snorted. 'Your wife has got her own pouch to carry wee Joey in.'

'Ah,' Super-Roo said. 'But my wife has had an accident. She tripped over a wombat and strained her pouch very badly. She can't carry little Joey in it any more. And now he thinks she doesn't love him.'

Dr McGurk looked grave. 'How verra sad,' he said.

'Yes, I'm terribly worried,' said Super-Roo. 'But a sporran could save us. If you would kindly give me your sporran, I could take little Joey hopping myself. That would give my wife's pouch a complete rest.'

Dr McGurk shook his head sadly. But he was only pretending. He had a very cunning idea. 'What a verra great pity!' he exclaimed. 'I would willingly give you my sporran, but I can't.'

'Why not?' asked Super-Roo.

'Because,' Dr McGurk said, 'the rules of the clan McGurk forbid any male McGurk to give his sporran away . . . or to sell it. *And,*' he added in a very solemn voice, 'the curse of the Great Monster of Loch Ness will fall on any robber who robs a male McGurk of his sporran. It is a verra frightful curse.'

'Oh, don't worry,' Super-Roo sniffed. 'I won't rob you of your sporran. I wouldn't stoop so low. I'm an upright kangaroo.'

'Och, aye,' said Dr McGurk. 'Well, I'm truly sorry about your poor sick wife and wee Joey. I would help them if I could. But if I've got to go, I've got to go.' He turned to Cathie, dozing by the water. 'Come on, up with you, Cathie. *Atcha, atcha, imshi!*'

'Stop, stop!' cried Super-Roo. 'I could call an extra special extraordinary meeting of the Council of Animals. I could ask them to make a new rule - about kindness to exhausted explorers.'

'Now, that's an idea!' said Dr McGurk.

'They probably won't do it,' Super-Roo said. 'But the dumbats and the numbats and the wombats and the skinks will argue about it for days and days. Maybe even weeks and weeks. While they're arguing, you and Cathie Khan can stay.' Then he added slyly: 'But of course you'll need my help.'

'Why?' asked Dr McGurk.

'Because I'll have to ask lots of questions to keep them talking,' explained Super-Roo. 'And I won't ask questions unless you *lend* me your sporran. You needn't give it, just lend.'

Super-Roo was just as cunning, in a kangaroo way, as Dr McGurk.

'Och, you drive a hard bargain,' said Dr McGurk. He cocked his head at Cathie Khan who blinked her beautiful brown eyes. Her long silky eyelashes glinted in the sun.

'Here's my sporran,' said Dr McGurk. 'I'll lend it to you, just for now.'

So Dr McGurk and Cathie Khan camped under the coolabah tree on the banks of the Willawallawalla Waterhole and rested. They had a wonderful holiday while the Council of Animals argued about them.

Cathie's humps grew bigger and bigger until they were back to their ordinary size. Dr McGurk practised playing his bagpipes, but he had to give it up because so many snakes came and hissed at him.

Every day Super-Roo visited the camp to tell Dr McGurk what was happening. One day he looked worried. 'I think the skinks are going to cross the floor of the House,' he said. 'That means they will vote to kick you out. The goannas have got at them.'

'I don't care,' said Dr McGurk. 'I'm getting bored. The sooner I leave here the better.'

'But I *do* care,' retorted Super-Roo. 'My wife's pouch isn't better yet. If you're so bored, what say I take you for a long hop?'

'Don't be silly,' Dr McGurk said. 'I wouldn't fit into my own sporran!'

'Forget about sporrans,' said Super-Roo. 'You can ride on my tail.'

The idea scared Dr McGurk, but he was too brave to show it.

'Och, aye,' he said. 'But watch out that you don't sprain your tail. I'm a braw, heavy man.' He climbed up on Super-Roo's tail and dug his knees in as hard as he could.

Super-Roo twirled the tip of his tail in the air and asked: 'Are you ready?'

'Och, aye,' said Dr McGurk. 'But be careful.'

'Hang on tight,' Super-Roo called. 'Get ready! Get set! Here...we...*go!*'

Super-Roo gave such a mighty hop that he didn't touch the ground for two kilometres. He simply whizzed through the air, with Dr McGurk hanging on and groaning: 'Oh, my gosh. Oh, my golly! Oh, grief and woe!'

'Hang on tighter,' Super-Roo cried. 'I'm coming in to land.'

And land he certainly did. *Ker-thump!*

Dr McGurk shot straight up about five metres into the air, turned head over heels four times and fell *ker-rash* into the middle of a brigalow bush.

At first Dr McGurk thought he was dead. Then he moved his arms and his legs and his neck and his fingers and his toes, one by one, very slowly to see if anything was broken. But it wasn't, so he knew he was only suffering from shock. He sat up.

Super-Roo bent down and put out a paw to help Dr McGurk stand up, but Dr McGurk was livid with rage.

'You mean, murdering marsupial, you!' he roared. 'You could have fractured my spine. Give me back my sporran this minute!'

'Don't get excited,' said Super-Roo soothingly. 'You're not hurt. How was I to know you couldn't ride?'

Dr McGurk was even more livid.

'I *can* ride, you great overgrown rat!' he bellowed. 'I'm a famous explorer. I can ride broncos and brumbies and donkeys and yaks and llamas. I can ride camels and elephants and greasy pigs . . . and goats because I'm a Freemason. I could even ride tigers if I didn't have to get off!'

'Well, I know one thing you can't ride and that's a kangaroo's tail,' said Super-Roo. 'Come on. Climb aboard again. I promise not to hop more than fifty metres at a hop.'

But Dr McGurk was still angry. 'Away with you, you blethering brute,' he said scornfully. 'I'll walk back.' And he did.

45

5

In which the Council of Animals Rule to Exterminate McGurk and his Camel, and Super-Roo has to do some Super-quick Thinking

The day after falling off Super-Roo's tail, Dr McGurk was sitting in the shade of the coolabah tree, singing a song about a ball that some Scottish people once had at a place called Kerrimuir, when Super-Roo came to talk.

'How are you this morning?' asked Super-Roo.

'As well as can be expected,' Dr McGurk said grumpily.

'I'm glad of that,' said Super-Roo, 'because I've got bad news for you. Last night the Council of Animals voted to expel you from this waterhole forthwith.'

'Poof!' said Dr McGurk. 'What do I care? I'm sick of it here, anyway.'

'But that's not the worst of it,' Super-Roo said. 'After the Council of Animals decided to expel you, they decided to exterminate you too. They passed a new rule called the *Extermination of Exhausted Explorers Act.*'

'Great grief!' exclaimed Dr McGurk. 'Murder and loot! Exterminate me? What harm have I done?'

'It's not the harm you *have* done,' Super-Roo explained. 'It's the harm you *will* do. Aren't you going to tell the whole world about discovering the Munga-longaloo Mountains in the dead centre of the Deadibone Desert?'

'Surely I am,' said Dr McGurk. 'What is the use of being a famous explorer if you can't say what you have discovered? I shall be given a Gold Medal and a Blue Certificate by the Royal Exploring Society.'

'Exactly!' Super-Roo said. 'You'll tell the world... and before a skink can wink, hundreds of human beings will be here dropping bits of orange peel and paper and bottles and empty cans and plastic bags. They will

pollute the whole place. The Willawallawalla Water-hole will be made so horrible that we will have to move out.'

'That's nonsense,' said Dr McGurk. 'People won't be able to get here without dying of thirst.'

'Pooh,' said Super-Roo. 'People can go to the moon these days. That's much harder than crossing the Deadibone Desert. Anyway, I am Head Animal and the chief executive of the Council of Animals and it is now my duty to exterminate you according to the Act.'

'How?' asked Dr McGurk. He could hear gurgles as Cathie Khan nervously pumped water round inside her.

Super-Roo looked sad. 'I suppose that the most merciful way,' he said, 'would be to turn the taipan snakes on you.'

Dr McGurk went deathly pale under his whiskers. 'But you couldn't!' he gasped. 'That would be inhuman!'

'I'm *not* human,' Super-Roo said. 'I don't *want* to exterminate you. I'm trying to think of some way of getting out of it.'

'Think hard,' said Dr McGurk. 'We won't interrupt you.'

Super-Roo thought and thought. Dr McGurk stood up very straight and Cathie tried to gurgle in silence.

At last Super-Roo said: 'I've got it! I think I can get

you out of it on a technicality. We might have to cheat a bit. But you will have to swear an oath on your Scotsman's word of honour that you will never tell anybody about discovering the Mungalongaloo Mountains and the Willawallawalla Waterhole.

'Hoots and toots!' protested Dr McGurk. 'Then I wouldn't get a Gold Medal and a Blue Certificate!'

'Suit yourself,' said Super-Roo. 'Which is worse... not getting a Gold Medal and a Blue Certificate or having the taipans turned on you?'

'Hum,' said Dr McGurk. 'Tell me about this technicality. How can it stop them exterminating me?'

'I'll tell you,' said Super-Roo. 'When the Council of Animals makes a new rule, it is not a real rule until the Head Animal has proclaimed it. That means it isn't a rule until I have hopped around and told everybody. It takes me two or three days if I don't hurry. You could escape in two or three days, couldn't you?'

'I surely could,' said Dr McGurk. 'I could escape now if you let me.'

'Not now,' said Super-Roo. 'I must not see you go or I would have to stop you. Wait until I have gone hopping to proclaim the rule. But first you must swear the oath.'

Dr McGurk held up his right hand and said: 'I do

hereby solemnly swear and declare that I will never tell anybody in the whole world that I have discovered the Mungalongaloo Mountains. On my Scotsman's word of honour!'

'Good,' said Super-Roo. 'There's one small thing . . . my wife's sprained pouch is still not better. You must leave me your sporran.'

'But I can't,' said Dr McGurk. 'The rules of the clan McGurk forbid me to give my sporran away or sell it. And don't forget the curse of the Great Monster of Loch Ness which will fall on anyone who steals it from me.'

'Super-Roo's whiskers twitched as if he grinned. 'But you won't be giving your sporran away . . . or selling it,' he said. 'I won't steal it from you. You can just leave it with me *on permanent loan.*'

Dr McGurk stared at Super-Roo with his mouth open in admiration. 'Well!' he said. 'You surely *are* a Super-Roo. I can understand why you are Head Animal at the Willawallawalla Waterhole. Och aye, you can have my sporran on permanent loan.'

Dr McGurk and Super-Roo shook hands solemnly.

'See you later,' said Super-Roo in a loud voice, and winked. He hopped off, four kilometres in one bound, with Dr McGurk's sporran dangling down in front of him.

In the middle of the night, Dr McGurk put on his snake-proof stockings, thorn-proof kilt, scorpion-proof trews, bush shirt, big shoes with nails in them, and his tam-o'-shanter with cork bobbles on top. He loaded up Cathie Khan very quietly and she got up without even a grunt or a gurgle. They disappeared like shadows into the Deadibone Desert, and left the Mungalongaloo Mountains and the Willawallawalla Waterhole behind them forever.

6

In which our Heroes Travel Long and Hard, to Return Triumphantly and Declare they Discovered Nothing (except a Secret)

On the way across the desert they had all sorts of hardships and adventures, but after forty-four days they came to the ghost-town of Gulgrumbalong. They were safe at last.

Gulgrumbalong has a population of four people. They all came out and shouted and clapped when Dr McGurk and Cathie Khan arrived.

PLIS SLOW DOWN!
you are now entering
GULGRUMBALONG
POP. 4 (PLUS FLIES) ELEVATION
MINUS 4 METRES

57

'What did you discover in the middle of the Deadibone Desert?' the people asked.

'Nothing,' said Dr McGurk. 'Nothing but its dead centre.'

About the Author

Osmar White is the author of many best-selling books on Australian and Pacific topics. He wrote the story of the Super-Roo for his three grandsons.

About the Illustrator

Jeff Hook is staff cartoonist at the *Sun News-Pictorial* in Melbourne. His work appears in many Australian newspapers. He has written and illustrated another book for children, *Jamie the Jumbo Jet*.

The Further Adventures of
Dr A. A. A. McGurk, M.D.

Osmar White
Illustrated by Jeff Hook

In these pages you will travel with the bravest explorer of
modern times, the great Alastair Angus Archibald McGurk and
his remarkable double-humped riding camel Cathie Khan whom
he teaches to ski so that together they can search for the fabled
Pole of Impossibility.

You will also meet a courageous hairy dog Trotsky, and a
wandering band of displaced animals led by a refugee from the
over-crowded tourist slopes of Mount Everest.

Why had they all gone to the ends of the earth? Were they to
survive trial by blizzard, fire and icequake? Or were they
swallowed up by a yawning crevasse or a fuming fumarole?

The Twenty-Seventh Annual African Hippopotamus Race

Morris Lurie
Illustrated by Elizabeth Honey

Bang! went the pistol.

Eighty-four champion hippopotamuses hit the Zamboola River. The crash was like thunder! It was the start of the Twenty-seventh Annual African Hippopotamus Race.

This is the eyewitness account of that great swimming marathon and a thrilling story of just what it takes to become a champion.

The Meeting Pool

Mervyn Skipper
Illustrated by R. W. Coulter

The animals of the jungle were worried. Each night, beside the meeting pool, they gathered to discuss how they could stop the White Man from chopping down the trees and destroying their home. Many were the ideas, and many were the stories told to illustrate them.

These stories are the folk tales of Borneo, re-told with wit, wisdom and delightful simplicity for quite small children, for their elder brothers and sisters and for parents and grandparents.

HEARD ABOUT THE PUFFIN CLUB?

. . . it's a way of finding out more about Puffin books and authors, of winning prizes (in competitions), sharing jokes, a secret code, and perhaps seeing your name in print! When you join you get a copy of our magazine, *Puffin Post*, sent to you four times a year, a badge and a membership book. For details of subscription and an application form, send a stamped addressed envelope to:

The Puffin Club Dept A
Penguin Books Limited
Bath Road
Harmondsworth
Middlesex UB7 oDA

and if you live in Australia, please write for your copy
of *Puffinalia* to:

The Australian Puffin Club
Penguin Books Australia Limited
P.O. Box 257
Ringwood
Victoria 3134